Kindergarrrten Bus

By Mike Ornstein

Illustrated by
Kevin M. Barry

Published by Sleeping Bear Press

EMERGENCY PLANK

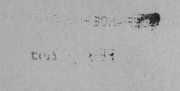

To me best mate, Fanny. I loves ye more than all the barnacles in the big blue sea!
—Mike

For Grayson, as he starts his kindergarten adventure.
—Kevin

Ahoy, boy!

What? It be ye first day of kindergarrrten?

Well, don't worry, laddie—
it be me first day as a bus driverrr!

Climb aboard!

All these little scoundrels back there be ye new mates.

But I be the captain of this here vessel!

And I run me a tight ship—*errr*, I mean bus.

So here be the rules.

No gettin' out of ye seats!

Raaaaa, mutiny!

That's right, Polly.

No yellin'!

Raaaaa, mutiny!

Keep ye hooks—*errr*, I mean hands—to ye self!

And always rrrespect ye mates!

"I miss my doggy."

"I miss my teddy."

"I miss my blankie."

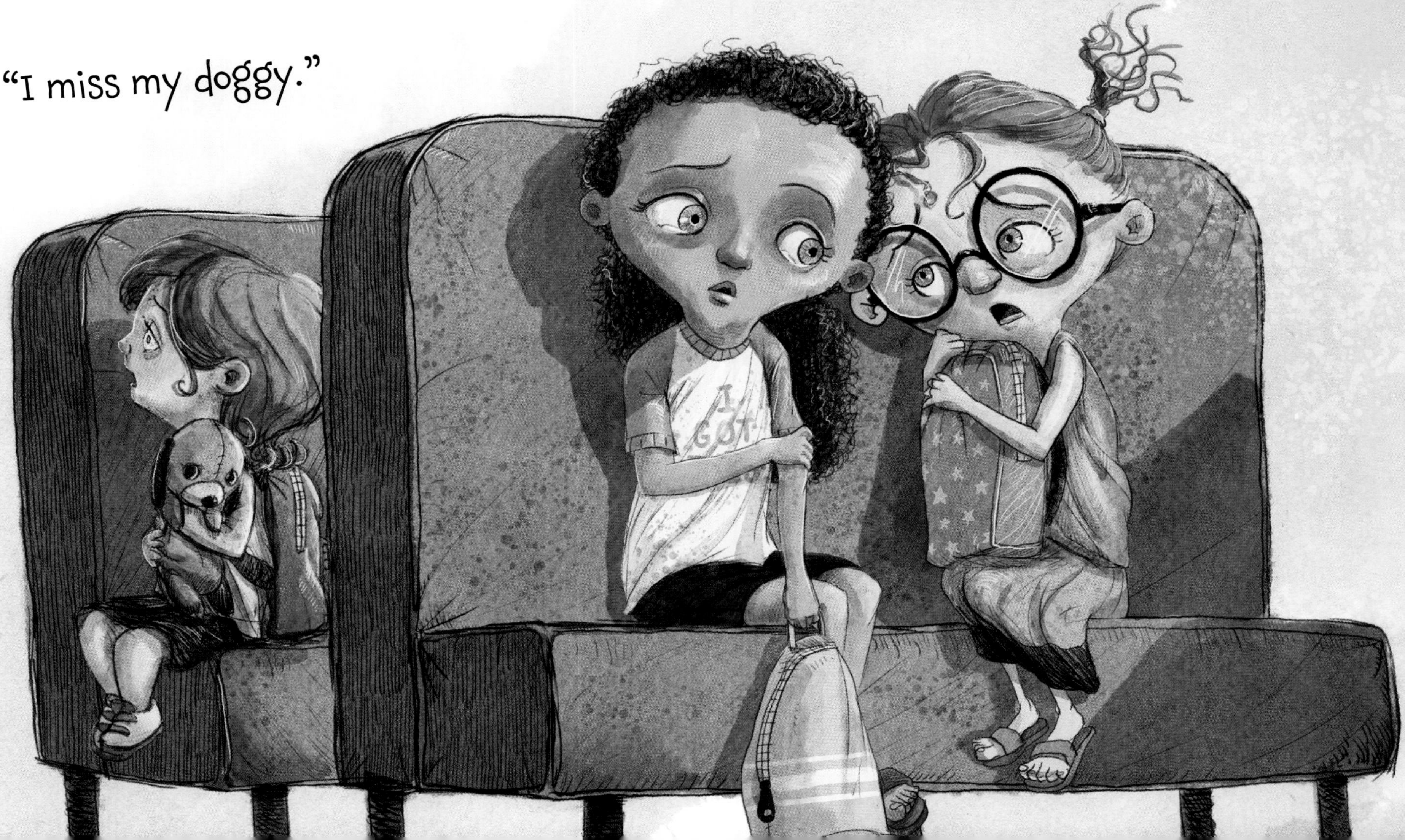

Arrrgh!

Pipe down, ye little landlubbers!

There'll be no blubberin' on me bus!

Pirates don't get scared! We eat bones for supperrr!

And we don't miss nobody neither!

'Cause we're rrrough! And we're tough!

And we ain't got time for that fluffy stuff!

Now hold me map, boy! **X** marks the spot where ye school be!

Shiver me timbers!

We've got rrrough seas—*errr*, I mean rrrough road—ahead!

Potholes . . . **arrrgh!** As far as me eye can see!

Batten down the hatches, me hardies!

Here we go!

I can't drive me bus without me sweet snuggly Polly!

I can't do it, I tells ya!

I can't! I can't! I can't!

"yes, you can!"

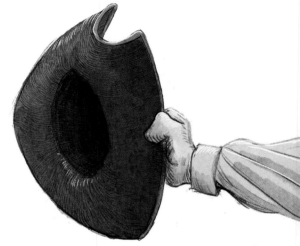

But I be scared without me Polly.

"Hey! I thought you said that pirates don't get scared."

"Yeah, and you said that pirates don't miss their mommies or doggies or anything either!"

I was only hornswogglin'.

Waaa arrrgh waaaa arrrgh!

I wanted ye to think I was brave
so ye would be brave too.

But I'm nothin' but a scared,
blubberin' boob of a buccaneer.

Waaaa arrrgh waaaa arrrgh!

Blimey!

Well, I'll be a barnacle on the back
of a blue-footed booby bird!

Let's get ye little scallywags
to kindergarrrten, then!
Now sing along, me hearties!

Thar she blows . . . School!

The treasure of all treasures!

Ye be learnin' to rrread and wrrrite.

Ye be playin' games and makin' new mates.

Ye be rrrunnin' around like scallywags durin' rrrecess.

Polly!

Ye followed the bus!

I knew ye wouldn't leave me!
I loves ye, Polly.

A Message to Pirates—ARRRGH!—Grown-Ups

Me name's Mike Ornstein. I be a grown man and I still gets anxious when me starts something new. Don't be judgin' me, arrrgh! New experiences be stressful for adults, too, ye know. Even tough guys like us pirates!

The way we deal with our own fears and uncertainty will have a huge impact on how our children confront theirs throughout their lives. So set the tone. Try to stay cool and be positive.

Young children need to know that it's natural to be nervous so they don't think they're alone in how they feel. Saying things like "Don't worry about it" or "Nothing's going to happen" is not realistic, and they will soon figure that out. Sometimes things *do* happen. One of our goals as parents and teachers is to prepare our children so they are as confident and ready for new experiences as they can be, and ready, too, for any "potholes" that get in their way!

If your child is anxious about starting something new—like kindergarten—familiarize them with what to expect. Role-play, act out different scenarios, read books, and make it fun! Visit a school classroom, if you can. Help them to think of all the positive things they will enjoy about their new adventure.

Next, find out what their worries are. Ask specific questions and listen to their answers. They may not be what you assume. This way, you can help them do some problem-solving and think of solutions. Empower them and ask what ideas they can come up with to feel better. Remind them about times when they were nervous and anxious in the past and got through them. Share your own experiences. And always make sure they know they have a safe and loving home to return to at the end of the day.

—Mike